Frédéric Stehr

QUACK-QUACK

A Sunburst Book · Farrar, Straus and Giroux

To Judith, Nachy, and Claire

"I see you, Fox! You can't fool me . . ." To protect her baby,
who will soon be hatching from its egg, Mama Duck teases Fox.

"You make too much noise, Fox. You're too slow. Try and catch me! Go on — jump!" Mama Duck leads Fox far from the nest, then flies away.

"Croak! Croak!" Little Frog jumps out of the pond and over to the nest. "Who could have left this egg?"

Crick . . . Crack . . .

"Quack! Quack!" The baby duck sees Little Frog. "Hello, Mommy!"

"No, Quack-Quack. I am not your mommy . . .

"Come with me. My mother will know where your mother is."

"Croak! Croak!" calls Little Frog. "Mommy, do you
know where Quack-Quack's mother is?"

"No," says Mama Frog. "But she looks like
Quack-Quack and she has feathers."

"Oh," says Little Frog. "Come, Quack-Quack.
I know someone who has feathers."

"Quack! Quack! Are you my mommy?"

"No, Quack-Quack. Your mother has white feathers and an orange beak like you," says Owl, taking Quack-Quack under her wing.

"Look over there! A bird with white feathers and an orange beak."

"Quack! Quack! Are you my mommy?"

"Honk! Honk! Honk! No, Quack-Quack. Your mother
has white feathers, an orange beak, and orange feet,"
says Swan, lifting Quack-Quack onto her back.

"Look!" cries Little Frog. "A bird with orange feet!"

"Honk! Honk! It has an orange beak," says Swan.
"Hoo! Hoo! It has white feathers," says Owl.
"Croak! Croak! It has orange feet," says Little Frog.

"Quack! Quack! Mommy!"

"Squawk! Squawk! No, little Quack-Quack," says Flamingo. "Your mother led Fox into the bamboo to keep him away from you."

"Don't go in there, it's too dangerous!" Little Frog cries.
"Stay with us. We'll protect you from Fox," says Owl.

"Mom-m-my! Mom-m-my!"
calls Quack-Quack.

"Help! Help!"

"Quack! Quack! Missed me! Quack! Quack!"

"Don't be afraid, Quack-Quack. Hold on tight, we're going home."
"Did you see, Mommy?
He's a silly fox.
He can't even fly!"

Mama Duck smiles. She can feel her baby still trembling with fear.
"I'll never leave you again," she says.